TIME RANGERS

5. A Toss of the Coin

As Worm entered the hut, the plan swung into action. He threw his weight against the door to force it wider and Ryan now had the target in his sights. His dead-ball blast from point-blank range couldn't have been more accurate. It hit the unsuspecting guard smack in the stomach, doubling him up in pain and making him retch.

The boys hauled the man inside, bolted the door and then bolted themselves. In the mad panic to escape, Ryan even forgot to retrieve the ball. Suddenly, another figure appeared in the dark in front of them.

Also in this series:

Look out for:

TIME RANGERS

5. A Toss of the Coin

Rob Childs

Hippo

GAZZA
GOALKEEPER — 1

WORM
RIGHT-BACK — 2

STOPPER
CENTRE-BACK — 5

RAKESH
RIGHT-MIDFIELD — 4

MR STOPPARD
MANAGER

JACKO
CENTRE-MIDFIELD — 8

SPEEDIE
RIGHT-WINGER — 7

RYAN
CENTRE-FORWARD — 9

ANIL
LEFT-WINGER — 11

MR THOMAS
MANAGER

For my wife Joy, with special thanks

Scholastic Children's Books,
Commonwealth House, 1–19 New Oxford Street,
London WC1A 1NU, UK
a division of Scholastic Ltd
London ~ New York ~ Toronto ~ Sydney ~ Auckland

First published in the UK by Scholastic Ltd, 1998

ISBN 0 590 19533 6

Typeset by DP Photosetting, Aylesbury, Bucks.
Printed by Cox & Wyman Ltd, Reading, Berks.

10 9 8 7 6 5 4 3 2 1

1 On tour

"I've always wanted to play against the Villa!" joked Ryan Thomas.

The Rangers' striker was gazing over the hedge at the small football pitch next to their campsite, eager for the soccer action to start.

"Hardly Villa Park, though, is it?" Dazza grunted. "I mean, just look at the state it's in. Grass is long enough to hide a herd of buffalo."

Ryan shrugged. "Perhaps it's not worth cutting it. Dad said a big road is being built soon, right across here. Everything's gonna be swallowed up."

As he spoke, two cars pulled off the country lane through a broken gate and bumped over the field towards the ramshackle changing hut.

"Must be some of the Solford Villa lads arriving at last," said Jacko, the captain of Tanfield Rangers. "Two hours after the visitors!"

"Gave us chance to put our tents up," smiled Dazza. "Great to be on tour again. Just like old times."

Jacko shuddered slightly, despite the warm August sunshine. "Don't mention old times. We had enough of those back at Easter."

They needed no reminding about the amazing events of Rangers' Easter tour of the Peak District. They'd gone there to play a few friendlies as an end of season treat, but some of the squad had found themselves involved in games that were definitely not on the scheduled fixture list.

"I still can't make any sense of all that weird time business," Ryan confessed. "Everybody knows time travel isn't possible."

"Yeah – until it happens," Jacko sighed. "Let's just hope it doesn't start up again now we've come away to the Cotswolds."

Dazza grinned. "We know one person who'd be happy if it did, eh? Worm even reckons the TR on our shirts ought to stand for 'Time Rangers'!"

The Rangers had been looking forward to this pre-season weekend tour, but none more so than Michael Winter, better known to his teammates as Worm. He'd been doing some historical research into the Cotswolds area during the summer holidays.

He knew that it was famous for the wool trade in the Middle Ages, but he was more interested in the earlier time of its Roman occupation. After checking through his own large collection of history books at home, he'd devoured most of the Roman Britain section in Tanfield library.

"It didn't take Worm long to find some history, did it?" Ryan muttered. "He almost wet himself on the bus just 'cos we were on the Fosse Way!"

The touring party had motored down the old Roman road that Friday afternoon in their two hired minibuses, driven by the team's joint managers, Mr Thomas and Mr Stoppard. No sooner had they turned into the campsite than Worm let out a screech and stuck his head out of the window.

"A dig! Look – over there. Towards the river."

Anil readjusted his eardrum and pulled Worm back in. "A what?"

"An archaeological dig," Worm enthused, his face alight.

The boys around them groaned. "Give

it a rest, will you, Worm?" said Stopper, the team's centre-back, as his dad switched off the engine. "History is banned, OK? School doesn't start for another week."

"What's a thingy-logical dig?" Anil whispered.

"Archaeological," Worm hissed back. "They're digging down in the ground to try and discover what was there in the past."

"So what are they looking for?"

"Dunno, but it's not going to take me long to find out," Worm grinned. "Bet it's got something to do with the Romans. There's loads of Roman stuff all over the Cotswolds."

The two-berth tent that Worm and Anil were sharing was the first one to be set up and Mr Stoppard came to check it was satisfactory. "Well done, smart work," he began and then paused. "Er, where's Michael?"

Anil raised his eyebrows. "I'll give you three guesses."

"Only need one," the manager replied with a frown, glancing towards the dig. "Go and fetch him back. Tell him there's some chores to do first and it won't be too long before kick-off."

Worm was already deep in conversation with one of the workers, an archaeology student in muddy jeans with his hair tied back in a pony-tail.

The boy's fertile imagination was in overdrive. "I can just picture the scene,"

he breathed in wonder. "Incredible to think I'm actually standing on the site of a real Roman villa!"

"Don't get carried away. You might not be," the man said. "We're pretty sure there was a large villa somewhere near the River Sol, but we don't know the exact location yet. And we're losing the race against time."

"How do you mean?" Worm asked, puzzled.

"We need evidence to prove the villa's existence. And if we can't find it by next week, then we won't be able to stop the new road taking this route," he said, looking dejected. "Not only will all this lovely countryside be spoiled, but centuries of our history will be bulldozed away and lost for ever."

Worm was horrified. That was the most terrible thing he'd ever heard. "Please can I do something to help?" he begged, his voice almost a whimper.

2 Toss-up

"Tails!" Jacko called out as the silver coin flipped through the air.

Three sets of eyes watched it land and roll round on the bare centre-spot. A bearded head glistened up at them in the evening sunlight.

"Funny looking bloke," Jacko said, picking up the coin to examine it more closely. "Who is it?"

"The Emperor Hadrian," the Solford Villa captain told him proudly. "Y'know, the one who built the wall up north. It's a real Roman coin."

"We found it a few years ago when we

returfed the goalmouth at the river end," said the referee, who was also Villa's coach.

"It brings us luck," claimed his side's skipper. "We'll kick towards the Sol as usual. We always score more in our lucky goal."

Jacko grinned. "The Rangers rely on skill, not luck."

"Just as well, 'cos this ain't gonna be your lucky day!" the boy sneered. "It might be our last game on here and we want a big win."

The match kicked off without Worm. The Rangers' regular full-back had been given a trowel to use at the dig and he'd lost all track of time. He had to be dragged away at the last minute to get changed. Ryan's dad, Mr Thomas, then decided to put his foot down and left Worm out of the starting line-up.

"Enough's enough, Michael," he fumed. "I got fed up at Easter with you wandering off by yourself somewhere and keeping us all waiting."

"Nobody else is interested in history like me," Worm said in his own defence, trying not to sulk.

"You and your history! I bet if you had the chance, you'd rather go and live in the past."

Worm didn't reply, but an exasperated Mr Thomas sensed what the boy's answer would be. The manager's mood did not improve when Rangers quickly found themselves two goals down, both as a result of dubious decisions by the referee.

The first looked offside and the second was a penalty awarded against Stopper for handball when the shot clearly struck his chest. It was soon nearly three, but Dazza managed to turn a close-range header over the bar.

"C'mon, mark up!" the goalkeeper screamed at his team. "That was a free header. You're letting this lot walk all over us."

The mishit corner went out of play and Mr Stoppard, acting as linesman, signalled a goal-kick. The referee, however, ruled that the ball had come off a Rangers' defender and gave another corner.

Mr Stoppard shook his head in amazement. "Looks like we're up against twelve men here," he muttered. "I've rarely seen such a biased ref."

"Aye, if we get a result out of this game, it'll be a minor miracle," said Mr Thomas bitterly.

The next corner was blocked by Stopper, careful to keep his hands well out of the way. He launched the ball upfield with a hefty boot, relieving some of his own frustrations into the bargain.

"Out, Blues, out!" he shouted.

The tourists, resplendent in their royal-blue kit with RANGERS splashed in white across their backs, moved up together to leave a couple of orange shirts in offside positions. As the ball dropped out of the sky to Ryan, the number nine failed to control it on the bumpy surface and his marker knocked it forwards once more.

"Offside, ref!" bellowed Mr Thomas from the touchline as his fellow manager instantly raised his flag. Both were ignored.

Villa's captain was clean through on goal, with time to take on the advancing Dazza himself or pass to an unmarked teammate. He was greedy. He tried to be too clever, wanting to show off his dribbling skills. The captain swayed and dummied this way and that, but Dazza was not to be distracted and kept his eyes firmly on the ball.

The goalie timed his dive to perfection, throwing himself at the striker's feet just inside the box to wrap his body bravely around the ball. The captain went

sprawling forwards full-length and for an awful, heart-stopping moment, Rangers thought the referee was going to whistle for another penalty. He certainly seemed tempted.

"Great save!" Jacko cried, slapping Dazza on the back. "That's showed 'em they can't get away with cheating all the time."

He made sure the referee heard his comment, knowing it would probably get him into trouble, which it did. The man gave him a stern lecture on dissent, but Jacko was satisfied that he had made his point on behalf of his team. Such blatant favouritism only made them even more determined to fight back and win the match – fairly and squarely.

By half-time, Rangers had not only managed to withstand the early battering, but had reduced the deficit to a single goal. Ryan, last season's leading scorer, had opened their new account with a stunning, low drive that fizzed into the net under the Villa keeper's dive.

"Well deserved, that goal," Mr Stoppard told the players at the interval. "You've really had to battle for any reward."

"You're not kidding," said Jacko. "They're a good enough team not to need extra help from their ref."

"Makes it all the better when we thrash 'em!" crowed Ryan.

"Don't count your chickens," his dad

warned. "Long way to go yet."

"Sure feels like it," said Anil, still breathing heavily. "That first half seemed endless."

"It's thirty-five minutes each way now, remember," said Mr Thomas. "You're all classed as under-thirteens this season."

The boys had not yet adjusted to their new status. "Not sure I like getting older," grinned Rakesh, eager to come on in midfield for the second half. "Everybody expects you to work harder – even at football!"

The Rangers were now better equipped to deal with their difficult task. They had a completely fresh right-hand side, with Worm and winger Speedie joining Rakesh to strengthen the team.

The changes had an immediate effect, although the equalizing goal came from a rare source indeed – Worm. The full-back had not put his name on the scoresheet at all the previous season.

More out of habit than with any harmful intent, he followed up Rangers' first attack as Rakesh sent Speedie scampering away along the right touch-line. His low cross into the middle was intercepted by a defender who stuck out a leg to prod the ball beyond the penalty area. Straight to where Worm was lurking.

Worm was surprised to find the ball suddenly appearing at his feet, but he now had an unexpected decision to make. Shoot or pass. In the end, he did neither.

Several teammates were demanding the ball, Ryan the loudest of the lot as always, making Worm all of a dither. As a Villa player rushed out to challenge him, he panicked and scooped the ball up into the air in the vague direction of the goal.

It looped over the heads of defenders

and attackers alike – and also out of reach of the flailing hands of the goalkeeper. The ball clipped the inside of the upright, high up just underneath the crossbar, and then dropped down to nestle comfortably in the bottom of the netting.

Worm flung his arms up in astonished delight. "I've scored! I've scored!" he whooped before he was engulfed by laughing Rangers.

"You beauty!" cried Rakesh into his ear. "What a jammy goal!"

"Placed it," Worm insisted, not bothered that nobody believed him. He floated back into position for the restart as if on a fluffy, white cloud. The Romans were forgotten – temporarily at least.

"Two–all. Reckon it's a toss-up which way it'll go now," Mr Thomas remarked. "We might yet even witness a miracle!"

3 Referee!

Worm's joy did not last long.

Five minutes after his goal, he put the ball into the back of the net again – only this time nobody ran to congratulate him. Trying to steer an awkward, bobbling cross to safety out of play, he miscued and sent the ball past a gaping Dazza.

"Brilliant!" exclaimed the goalkeeper sarcastically. "Once this boy starts scoring, you can't stop him!"

"Forget it, Worm," Jacko said generously. "Just get on with the game."

That's exactly what Rangers did. They

resumed their attacks on Villa's "lucky" goal in search of another equalizer, but it took a quarter of an hour of incessant bombardment before the breakthrough came. Jacko was dominating the mid-field, at the heart of all their best moves, and it was the captain himself who levelled the scores once more.

Ryan set it up. He leapt to head a centre from Anil down to Jacko and the ball was struck fiercely on the volley

before it hit the ground. The keeper was quite glad not to be in the way of the screaming missile.

The Villa defending became more and more desperate after that as they scrapped hard to hold out for the final whistle. Their tackling was wild and crude at times, with Anil and Speedie on the wings receiving the roughest treatment. The referee turned a blind eye to most of the fouls and the Rangers' own tempers were wearing dangerously thin.

"I can't believe this guy!" Ryan stormed as the referee again waved play-on after Speedie was clumsily bowled over by his marker. "He's letting his team get away with murder."

"He'd probably just say it was in self-defence!" Jacko muttered.

"He's looking at his watch now," Rakesh pointed out as he jogged by. "Bet he'll blow up early to try and save them from defeat."

"Don't let's give him chance," said Jacko and clapped his hands to rally his team. "C'mon, big effort. There's still time for a winner."

The captain led by example. He gained possession of the ball on the half-way line and then switched play out to the left wing. The scything pass sent the gangly Anil off on a loping run that took him past one challenge before he cut inside for goal. He was about to shoot when his legs were swept from under him by a late tackle from behind.

"Penalty!" screamed every Rangers' player except Anil. He'd had all the breath knocked out of him.

Even the referee had to agree that it was a foul. "Direct free-kick," he announced. "It was outside the area."

"C'mon, ref!" Ryan cried. "Everybody could see that was well inside the box. It's got to be a pen."

"Don't argue with me, lad, or I'll send

you off," the man snapped, glaring at him. "Free-kick is all you're going to get."

Jacko pulled Ryan away. "No good wasting your breath. We can still punish them from here. Let's have one of your specials."

Few people their age could strike a dead ball as well as Ryan. He spent hours practising free-kicks and sometimes it paid off in a match. He wound himself up for a blockbuster.

Villa's defensive wall of bodies looked about as stable as the leaning tower of Pisa. It seemed on the point of collapse as Ryan ran in and then at the last second one boy lost his nerve and ducked away. His action might have saved him from being decapitated as the ball powered right through the gap he'd left in the wall.

The shot thundered into the upright, causing the whole framework of the goal

to shudder to its foundations. Speedie was the first to react as the ball rebounded back into play and he instinctively swung his boot at it.

He connected so sweetly that the net was billowing out before anybody realized what had happened. When they did, the winger was lifted off his feet in celebration and virtually carried back to the half-way line.

"You've had the last laugh after all

their fouling," yelled Rakesh.

"That's the best way to answer them back," grinned Jacko. "Hit them where it hurts – in the back of the net!"

"Concentrate!" shouted Mr Thomas. "It's not over yet."

"It is now!" Jacko decided. "Villa have had it."

Jacko was right. There was no way back for Villa, despite the referee mysteriously finding many long minutes of added time on his watch. Eventually he had to give up, resigned to his side's 4–3 defeat.

The Rangers' managers didn't speak to the referee afterwards about his poor handling of the match. They feared they might well say something that they'd regret. They were full of praise, however, for their team.

"Wonderful comeback, boys," beamed Mr Stoppard. "Augurs well for the new season, showing guts and character like that."

Mr Thomas agreed. "Pleased you all kept trying to play football the right way; well done. We're proud of you."

It was a happy Rangers' party that collected their towels from the tents and trailed off to the shower block. Worm took the scenic route, pausing by the wooden palings that fenced off the dig. The archaeologists had packed up their tools and gone home.

"Hope they can find the villa before it's too late," he murmured as he gazed at the site in the golden sunset over the River Sol. He shook his head in sorrow at the thought of all that history being buried under tonnes of concrete and motorway.

Worm was to spend a restless night in the tent. He tossed and turned in his sleeping-bag, waking a grumbling Anil several times by crying out in his dreams. They were more like nightmares. He and his teammates were being kept as slaves in a Roman villa. And the slave-driver who was beating them bore an uncanny resemblance to the Solford referee!

The Saturday in-between Rangers' two matches was planned as a day out for the squad. In the August heat, the boys were nearly all togged out in their own soccer kit, some of them stripped to the waist with shirt tied around their middle.

For Worm at least, this was the highlight of the Cotswolds weekend – a sightseeing tour of the local area in and around Cirencester, once known as Corinium, the second largest town in Roman Britain. His teammates were looking forward more to ending the day in the swimming pool.

They thought of that treat now as they traipsed wearily around the extensive ruins of Chedworth Roman Villa. Especially when they peered into the cold plunge room of the well preserved, main bathhouse.

"Wish that was still full of lovely cold water," said Ryan. "I'd be in it like a flash."

"I'd prefer a nice long soak in a hot bath myself," ventured Speedie. "These bruises on my legs are dead sore."

"Received in the line of duty!" laughed Stopper. "And you're not the only one. Bet some of the Villa lads are licking their wounds as well this morning. What a game!"

Jacko pointed across to where the hypocaust central heating system had been excavated. "Look at Worm going mad with his camera. He must have got through a whole film already."

"If I know Worm, he'll be wishing he could see the villa like it used to be when the Romans were here," observed Stopper.

The captain frowned. "With him, it won't just be wishful thinking either. He knows it could really happen."

"I think we're tempting fate coming to a place like this," said Dazza. "I'm trying to stay as far away from Worm as possible, just in case."

"We all are," said Stopper. "I don't want to get dragged back into the past again. The Romans would give us more than just a few bruises!"

4 Over and over

After a picnic lunch, Worm wandered round the Corinium Museum in Cirencester by himself, a good way behind the others. He didn't mind. He was too absorbed in studying all the information on display about Roman Britain, especially the rooms with wonderful models and mosaic floors.

In the end, Mr Thomas had to hurry Worm through to the exit. "C'mon, lad, get a move on. We've still got the Roman amphitheatre to go to yet."

The interest of the footballers perked up for this visit. They expected something like the famous Colosseum in Rome where the gladiator and animal fights took place.

"Is this it?" said Dazza in disappointment when they reached the site. He gazed up at the undulating, grassy mounds that now covered the banks of seating around the oval arena. "Not much to see."

"Looks like they haven't excavated it properly yet," said Mr Stoppard.

"Have to tell those thingy-ologists to come here instead," said Anil. "At least they'd know where to start digging."

"You can still imagine what it must have been like at the games," said Rakesh. "Huge crowds screaming for blood!"

"Yeah, all them slaves and criminals torn to bits by wild animals," put in Ryan with an evil grin. "Great fun!"

"Yes, thank you, Ryan, I think we've got the picture," said his dad. "If you lot are going to get all bloodthirsty, you can take it out on each other while Mr Stoppard and I enjoy a little snooze in the sun."

"Good idea," said his fellow manager before issuing a warning. "Not *too* rough, mind. We don't want any injuries. You've got another match to play tomorrow, remember."

The lads organized the mock battles themselves. Skins versus tops. The bare-chested brigade and the soccer shirts charged from the two entrances to clash and grapple noisily in the centre of the arena. A kill was claimed whenever somebody was hauled over into the long grass.

A series of single-combat wrestling matches followed, cheered and jeered by the raucous supporters on the banks. Ryan and Stopper each won their way through three contests.

"The Grand Final!" announced Jacko. "A fight to the death!"

The two friends eyed one another warily. They had too much mutual respect to ever risk engaging in a real fight, but they had a certain reputation to protect in front of all their mates.

"Just pretend stuff, no punches, OK?" said Ryan.

"Agreed. But let's put on a good show for the crowd, eh?"

They began circling menacingly, half-crouched, arms outstretched, waiting for the right moment to make their first move. Suddenly Ryan lunged forward, but Stopper dodged to the left and his opponent grabbed at thin air. Ryan lost both his balance and his dignity.

"Not very graceful," Stopper teased him. Then he launched an attack of his own, finding a grip around Ryan's bare shoulders and trying to use brute strength to force him down to the ground. He met stubborn resistance. Ryan dug his trainers into the turf and almost succeeded in twisting Stopper over his back.

The two combatants broke apart, breathing heavily. Their smiles had gone. Neither wished to be shown up.

After much feinting and jousting for position, they locked horns again and Ryan managed to wrap a leg around Stopper's calves. He strove mightily to topple him backwards but Stopper clung on, employing his greater weight and

slight advantage in height to make Ryan ease the pressure of his hold. Something had to give – and it did.

A hidden pothole in the grass was Ryan's undoing. As his foot slipped, his grip slackened off and Stopper seized the opportunity. He deftly shifted his stance and wrestled Ryan towards the floor, but then found himself tumbling over too. Ryan had clutched a handful of shirt collar as he fell and they heard a loud rip as they dragged each other down.

Their laughing teammates ran from the slopes to join them. "An honourable draw!" Jacko declared.

"Let's have a rematch," cried Rakesh.

"No way!" gasped Ryan, sitting up. "I'd rather fight a lion!"

Stopper wasn't listening. He'd pulled off his shirt and was busy inspecting the collar. "Look what you've gone and done," he complained loudly. "It's almost torn off."

"Soz," Ryan murmured, secretly admiring the damage. "Didn't mean to."

"They cost a bomb, these do. Dad won't buy me another."

"It's out of date, anyway," Speedie laughed. "You can tell him you need a new one to keep up with the latest design."

Stopper brightened a little. "Hmm, good thinking. If I don't wear it, he may not notice."

"They weren't even watching your fight," said Jacko. "Just look at them two sleeping beauties up there!"

"How about a game of footie now?" Ryan suggested. "The ball's next to Dad. I'll go and get it."

"Don't bother," Rakesh told him. "It's too hot."

The squad split into two. Those who wanted to have a kickabout and those who preferred to sunbathe. Worm didn't wish to do either. He wandered to the top of the highest mound to soak in the atmosphere of the amphitheatre, conjuring up scenes in his mind's eye of the great Roman spectacles that must have been staged there.

He was so lost in his day-dreams that a sudden attack caught him completely off guard. His shirt was pulled off his back and he only just managed to hang on to his shorts. "Get off! Leave me alone."

His four tormentors laughed at his flash of temper. "OK, OK, Worm. Keep your hair on," cackled Ryan. "And your shorts!"

"You looked so lonely up here by yourself, we thought you might like a spot of company," Dazza grinned.

"I bet you did," Worm grunted. "Just come to annoy me, more like. Got bored playing football, have you?"

"Rakky's right. It *is* too hot," said Stopper, tossing the ball into Ryan's hands and slumping next to Worm.

Jacko felt tempted by the long, inviting slope down the other side. "Hey, you guys fancy a roly-poly race? Haven't done that for years."

The response wasn't too enthusiastic, but the captain persuaded them into action. "C'mon, just the once. Last one to the bottom's a wimp!"

Grumbling, they took up the challenge. The five boys spaced themselves along the banking, giving each other

plenty of room to lie flat out. At a signal from Jacko, they pushed away and began rolling bumpily downwards, arms tucked in or stretched out, according to style. Ryan even kept tight hold on the football.

Over and over ... blue sky ... green grass ... over and over ... blue ... green ... blue ... green ... over and over...

Worm came dizzily and abruptly to a halt. Disorientated, he wondered if he'd rolled way off course as there was now gravel underneath him, not grass. As his senses returned, he realized his face was pressed up against a man's hairy legs with heavy, strapped sandals on his smelly feet.

Worm tried to get to his knees but was pushed roughly back on to the hard ground, grazing his elbow. "Oi! What d'yer think you're doing?" he cried out, then looked up at the figure for the first time.

The man yelled something at him, but Worm was too shocked to understand a single word. It wouldn't even have mattered if Worm had his full wits about him. He'd never studied Latin at school.

Standing over him, and thrusting a short, broad sword towards his bare ribs, was an armoured Roman soldier. Just like the one he'd seen in the museum. Only this one looked to be in a very bad mood.

5 For sale

The Roman soldier grabbed Worm by the hair and hauled him to his feet. He shook the frightened boy fiercely and spat out what sounded like questions, but Worm hadn't a clue how to answer them.

The man gave up and slammed him against the wall of a high building. Worm had the unmistakable impression that he was expected to stay right where he was.

Then he gasped in horror. All four of his friends had met the same fate. Grazed and confused, they were being dragged towards him by other soldiers. Dazza's nose was pouring with blood.

"What the hell's happened to us?" Ryan demanded.

"I think we know what's happened," Jacko hissed. "No prizes for guessing where we've ended up this time. Thanks a bunch, Worm."

"Not his fault," Stopper defended him. "It was your idea to go rolling about, remember."

"We've really had it now," Dazza groaned, trying to stop his nosebleed. "They're gonna kill us for sure."

"No, they won't," said Stopper. "Not in front of all these people."

The boys' sudden appearance and capture had briefly made them the centre of interest. Passers-by were staring at the huddle of half-naked bodies before moving on to go about their business. There didn't seem to be any chance of escape. The soldiers were keeping a wary eye on them, discussing what to do. Worm tried to assess their situation.

"If time travel is working like it's done before, we must still be at the amphitheatre," he reasoned. "In those days, it stood outside the walls of Corinium. Er ... *these* days, I mean. Saw diagrams of it in that museum."

"Wish I'd taken more of an interest in there myself now," Jacko sighed. "I feel so helpless not being able to explain things to the soldiers."

"As they can't get any sense out of us, they perhaps think we're from some distant part of the Empire," said Worm. "Watch out! It looks as if they've come to a decision. Just act stupid."

"That should be easy enough," muttered Dazza.

Two of the soldiers approached and urged them all to stand up. The leader pointed to the right with his sword and shoved Ryan in the back.

"OK, OK, we're going," Ryan protested uselessly. "No need to push."

"Just hope they're not taking us inside the amphitheatre," said Jacko. "I don't reckon they'd be giving us free tickets for the stand."

"More likely a close-up view of the lions," Dazza said grimly.

"I think we're heading for the gates into the town," said Worm. "Being taken in for further questioning, I expect."

"Oh, shame!" Ryan exclaimed. "Just when I've gone and left my Latin phrase book in the tent. Don't suppose they'd let me nip back and get it."

He was still in defiant possession of the football, though. For Ryan, life would hardly be worth living without that!

The travellers were herded through the busy streets into the market-place, an open, colonnaded square at the centre of town.

"This is the forum," Worm said as they gazed around the shop-lined area. "All Roman towns were designed with the same layout."

"Fascinating!" Ryan sneered. "I bet you're almost enjoying this."

That was an unfair accusation. Especially when they were soon bound together with chains around their arms and made to stand in line with a number of other captives. An animated crowd began to gather and several men dressed in loose, white togas came forward to inspect them more closely. One prodded their chests and backs and then squeezed them on the arms to feel their muscles.

"Anybody would think he was looking to buy us," Ryan muttered as the man moved off further down the line. "It's like a cattle market."

Worm's heart sank as he realized what was taking place. "More of a slave market, I'm afraid. We *are* up for sale.

To be sold to the highest bidder as slaves."

"What! They can't do that to us!" gasped Dazza. "It's ... barbaric!"

"They can do what they want," Jacko murmured, equally appalled. "Our only hope is that we might be sold as a job lot and stay together."

"We've got more muscle and flesh on us than the rest of these poor blokes," said Stopper. "And we're much younger."

"Well, we'd better fetch a good price, then," Ryan growled. "Good footballers are worth millions nowadays!"

"Not in Roman times, they weren't," said his captain. "Bet they don't even know what that thing is under your arm. It's been getting some very strange looks."

After constant, degrading manhandling, the boys felt like little more than meat. Even their mouths were forced open for their teeth to be examined. What made matters worse was that they could understand nothing that was being said about them. It was all of a babble.

They knew when it was their turn, however, once the auction started. They were pushed forward as a group and the bidding seemed to be livelier and continue longer than for the other slaves. Finally, a fat, balding man in the crowd appeared well pleased with his purchases and summoned help to collect his wares. Three men in plain brown tunics ran forward and led the boys immediately out of the forum into the streets again.

"At least we got our wish. We've been kept together," said Stopper. "Could have been worse, I guess."

"Not much worse," Ryan scowled, jangling his chains. "Who are these guys we're with now?"

"Fellow slaves, most likely," said Worm. "Ones trusted by the master."

"Perhaps we can try and bribe them to let us go."

"What with? That football!" scoffed Dazza.

"More than their lives are worth to disobey the master," said Jacko. "They'd probably be killed if they allowed us to escape."

"Brilliant! So how are we gonna get out of this mess?" Ryan demanded.

Nobody had any answer to that. Not even Worm.

Nor did they have any idea where they were being taken. They passed out of the gates and Corinium was soon left far behind. The party slogged along well-made roads and dusty trackways for hours, trekking deep into the country-side, and it was dark long before they arrived at their destination.

The footsore, dispirited travellers were bundled into a hut, and they collapsed on to heaps of straw, still chained together.

Despite their exhaustion, sleep was slow to claim them, their troubled minds not eased by the sound of rats rustling about in the straw.

Each boy woke up more than once in the night, feeling cold and hungry – and desperate to go to the toilet!

6 Villa life

"Where are we?" Stopper murmured groggily as daylight began to filter through small cracks in the walls of the windowless hut.

He attempted to stretch, but the restrictions of the chains around his arms brought back with a jolt the full horror of their plight. Ryan next to him was already awake.

"Not in a five-star holiday camp, that's for sure," he grunted. "It's probably that fat Roman's villa. Y'know, like the one at what's-its-name."

"Chedworth," Worm piped up.

"That'd be funny, if we've turned up there after we saw it in ruins yesterday."

"Oh yeah, hilarious!" Dazza snapped. They'd all woken up now. "If somebody doesn't let us out soon, I'm gonna have to disgrace myself."

"Not while we're still linked up together, you're not," Jacko told him flatly. "You'll just have to hold it like the rest of us."

They heard the door being unbolted and pushed ajar. Bowls of porridge and bread crusts appeared in the shaft of light before the door was closed and fastened once more. Breakfast did not prove very appetizing and most of it was left for the rats.

When the bolt scraped again, the door was thrown wide open. A robed figure was framed in silhouette for several seconds and then the figure barked a command at them. Instinctively, they scrambled clumsily to their feet and were ushered outside.

"How are we supposed to know what to do when we can't follow what anybody says," hissed Jacko.

"No need to be worried about being overheard," Stopper said in a normal voice. "They can't understand us either."

"But this is England," said Ryan. "Surely some of 'em can speak English besides all this stupid Latin stuff?"

"Don't think the English language has been invented yet," said Stopper. "That right, Worm?"

Worm nodded, too intent on trying to take in their new surroundings. The view looked vaguely familiar, with a river glinting beyond the fields, but he was certain they weren't at Chedworth.

The farm manager studied them sternly, judging their worth, and the boys fell silent. They were grateful that he directed one of the slaves in attendance to release the chains that had so

badly chafed their arms. The grey-haired man pointed to each of the new recruits in turn, spoke sharply and then strode away, leaving the slaves to carry out his orders.

The travellers were shown first to a latrine hut. Its purpose was clear both from the smell and the circular holes cut side by side along the length of a low, wooden bench.

"Well, this is cosy," muttered Jacko.

"No privacy round here."

"Quite hygienic, though," Worm grinned. He picked up a sponge on the end of a stick from out of a water channel running across the stone floor. "I'll leave you to work out for yourselves what these are used for. Just make sure you wash them out properly afterwards!"

Back outside, they were handed clean brown tunics that came down almost to their knees. All the slaves were dressed the same – apart from their own incongruous trainers.

"See you later – with a bit of luck," Jacko said as they were split up. "Keep your eyes open and we'll start making some escape plans tonight."

Ryan and Stopper had been specially chosen for their stronger builds to labour in the fields, helping with the harvest. It was back-breaking work in the hot sun, but at least they were able to size up the local area, assessing possible escape routes.

Jacko spent the day among a group of slaves fetching water from the river in heavy jugs. As he rested briefly on the bank, he stared in sudden shock at the wide, sweeping bend of the river around a rocky outcrop. A chill tingle slithered down his spine like a snake.

"It must be, surely!" he gasped and then began to chuckle. "Can't wait to tell Worm his precious archaeologists are digging in the wrong place!"

On his weary journeys to and fro, however, Jacko was never close enough to speak to anybody. He picked out Ryan and Stopper in the distance at times, saw Dazza collecting firewood and stoking the furnaces that heated the bathhouse, but he only caught one glimpse of Worm inside the kitchen.

"Typical!" he grunted, staggering under the weight of the water vessel.

"Worm's gone and landed the cushy job all right."

Worm did not quite see it that way. With its open, charcoal-fired stove, the kitchen felt like one huge oven. And some of the items being prepared for the family's meals made his stomach churn. The snails and doves he thought were bad enough, but when it came to the stuffed dormice!

Where Worm had fallen lucky was in having the company of a friendly slave-cook, not much older than himself, by the name of Marcus. He helped Worm keep the cooking fire going in the hearth and showed him how to wash and prepare the various vegetables and herbs. Worm was a quick learner and they communicated well enough through gestures and the pulling of funny faces to make each other laugh.

For the final meal of the day, Worm was even allowed to serve in the dining-

room. He took round a water bowl for the diners to clean their fingers in between the many lavish courses. With the fat owner at the head of the low table, the guests lounged on long, padded couches to enjoy the feasting and listen to music.

Worm was so absorbed in witnessing at first hand the kind of scene he'd only read about in history books, he almost failed to spot the small silver coin lying on the tiled floor mosaic. It was too good an opportunity to miss. Worm let the towel drop from his grasp and as he bent to pick it up, coolly slipped the coin inside one of his shoes.

Guard-slaves escorted the boys back to their sleeping hut for the night, with Worm the last to arrive. He decided it was best not to tell his mates what he was called in the kitchen – Wormus!

"Here he is!" snorted Ryan. "Been scoffing food all day long, I bet."

"There's a few pickings, sure," Worm admitted, "but most of it is too spicy for my taste. The wine to wash it down wasn't too bad, though!"

They heard the bolt being slid into position again, leaving them in darkness.

"Still don't trust us, do they?" Jacko muttered.

"Can't say I blame them," said Stopper. "First chance we get, I vote we leg it fast and try and get back to that amphitheatre."

"Dead right," Ryan agreed. "On the

other trips, we've always had to return to the same place we came through to travel back to our own times."

"As long as we're all together," Jacko insisted. "We don't want to leave anybody behind."

Ryan's wicked grin was lost in the gloom. "Oh, I don't know..."

"Ignore him, Worm, he's only joking," said Jacko, eager to break the news of his amazing discovery. He'd been nearly bursting, waiting for Worm to reappear. "It's a pity we can't just slip back to camp from here..."

"How d'yer mean?" urged Dazza. "C'mon, have you found a short-cut?"

"No, but at least I do know where we are..." whispered Jacko teasingly.

"Where?" they demanded.

"...Solford Villa!" he exclaimed loudly and delighted in the stunned reaction of his audience. "I knew you'd all be gobsmacked!"

Once Jacko had convinced the others he was right, they could have kicked themselves for not realizing, too. Especially Worm. "We've got to get back to the future," he stressed. "We can save the villa now."

"Save the environment, too," Stopper reminded him. "No trees or anything would have to be destroyed to make way for that new road."

"I'd love to hear you try and explain to the archaeologists how we found out where the villa is!" chortled Ryan.

"Right now, though, it's not exactly a big help knowing we're at Solford," Stopper pointed out. "We're more concerned about getting away from it."

"There's always too many other people about," said Jacko. "And the only time we're all together is when we're locked in here."

"No chance of escaping in broad daylight, in any case," said Worm.

"We'd easily get recaptured. That's why it's got to be at night. Listen, meals are not the only things I've been cooking up in the kitchen..."

They liked the sound of the main ingredients of Worm's plan. They then added their own ideas to it, stirred it round for a while and decided to put it on the following night's menu.

7 Escape bid

Worm and Marcus left the kitchen together when their duties ended. It had been another hot, uncomfortable day's work, but they'd enjoyed some light-hearted moments, too. Worm could still taste the snail that Marcus had tricked him into eating.

Marcus sensed his new friend's excitement. He'd caught Worm's eye more than once during the evening and knew that something was about to happen. He could guess what it probably was, too. Marcus had been wanting to escape himself ever since being brought to the villa as a slave a year ago.

They looked at each other and nodded in understanding. No words needed to pass between them. As a guard took him back to the hut, Worm signalled Marcus to wait. He knew the other Rangers would already be in position.

As Worm entered the hut, the plan swung into action. He threw his weight against the door to force it wider and Ryan now had the target in his sights. His dead-ball blast from point-blank range couldn't have been more accurate. It hit the unsuspecting guard smack in the stomach, doubling him up in pain and making him retch.

The boys hauled the man inside, bolted the door and then bolted themselves. In the mad panic to escape, Ryan even forgot to retrieve the ball. Suddenly, another figure appeared in the dark in front of them.

"Leave this to me!" cried Stopper. "I'll deal with him."

"No!" Worm hissed. "It's only Marcus."

"Who the hell's Marcus?" exclaimed Ryan.

"He's my friend in the kitchen. I think he's coming with us."

Marcus jumped at the chance. Ryan and Stopper set a fast pace, leading the way through the fields and up a hill towards the woods. Loud voices raised the alarm behind them. They hadn't got the kind of head start they'd hoped for.

"Told you we should have gagged that guard," cried Ryan.

"We've still got the advantage of surprise," panted Stopper, charging up the steep slope. "We'll take some finding in these woods."

They were unlucky. Unknown to them, the farm manager had taken a group of slaves that day to help gather the harvest on a smaller, neighbouring villa. They were returning along the trail through the woods when the fugitives ran right into them.

There was a fierce scuffle and blows were exchanged with the older slaves, but it was an unfair struggle. The boys were outnumbered and unarmed. A blade flashed in the moonlight.

"Watch out! He's got a knife!" yelled Jacko.

He hurled himself at the manager just as he was about to plunge it into

Dazza's back. The man was knocked off balance and the knife looped away into the undergrowth. Even so, he twisted round and punched Jacko to the ground while the others were also overpowered. They were marched back out of the woods into the arms of a posse from the villa.

"Thanks for saving my life," gasped Dazza as they were jostled along.

"Makes us all square," Jacko grunted, referring to a previous time adventure

when Dazza had rescued him from certain death.

It was only as they were chained together once more in the hut that people realized that one of the new slaves was still missing.

Stopper glanced round at his bewildered pals. "Where's Worm?"

In all the confusion in the woods, Worm had been grabbed from behind and pressed face down into the undergrowth to prevent him crying out. He thought he was going to be suffocated until he heard a voice in his ear.

"Wormus!"

He stopped struggling and was allowed to wriggle over on to his back. By the time it was reported to the manager that Marcus the cook had also disappeared, the two runaways were well hidden in the leafy branches of a tall tree. It seemed the safest place while the hunt was on.

When they heard a search party scouring beneath them among the trees, Marcus put a finger up to his lips, then relaxed as the men moved away. They grinned at each other and gave the thumbs-up sign.

Wedged securely in the thick branches, Worm closed his eyes and tried to doze, fearful of what the new day might bring. Even if Marcus wanted to leave the area, Worm knew he must remain and seek some way of releasing his friends – if they were still alive.

Worm awoke with a start to find himself alone. He panicked for a moment, wondering where he was, and then panicked some more when he remembered. The chill light of dawn was breaking through the foliage and he felt desolate. He hated the thought that the others might think he had deserted them to save his own skin.

Worm tensed as he heard somebody climbing up the tree, but was greeted by that familiar, friendly smile. Marcus had brought a breakfast of fruit. They ate in companionable silence and then the cook beckoned him to follow. Worm was too stiff to budge at first, but with a helping hand, he clambered slowly down the tree trunk and dropped the last metre or so to the ground.

Soon he was trailing Marcus through the trees, skirting the edge of the wood overlooking the villa and the road in the valley below. Worm peered down and gasped, tugging at the cook's tunic and pointing.

Marcus grinned and Worm realized that he must already have known what was happening. Keeping low out of sight, they strained to make out more details. There were a couple of horse-drawn carts on the road with people aboard, including the fat owner, and a number of slaves

walking alongside. Behind them, chained to the rear cart, were four stumbling, bare-backed figures.

"Corinium?" Worm murmured and Marcus nodded, jabbing a finger at his own chest at the same time. That's where he was making for too. Now he was free, he planned to start a new life for himself in the town as a cook.

They followed the procession at long range, checking constantly for any threat of ambush. As the miles between them and the villa increased, they felt more confident, but still kept to the woodland and ditches.

Their caution was justified. A cohort of Roman soldiers came marching along the stone-paved road away from the town. They made a spectacular sight. The sunlight glinted off their helmets and shields while their metal-studded sandals crashed down in unison, sending great swirls of dust up into the air.

As the walls of Corinium came into view, the road became more crowded and they joined the throngs of excited people. The amphitheatre loomed up ahead and Worm's growing fears for the fate of his friends were confirmed. This must be a day when the Games were being staged!

He and Marcus mingled with the milling thousands around the stalls and sideshows outside the stadium. They did not look too much out of place. Many slaves were among the townspeople and merchants, busy taking messages and doing jobs for their masters.

Peeping through a gap between two stalls, Worm saw the Rangers slumped against the cart, too exhausted to stand up but unable to sit and rest because of their chains. They looked bruised and battered after their tortuous trek. Worm hoped for their sakes that they hadn't yet realized what had been decided would be a fitting punishment for their crime.

Worm watched as the boys were separated from the cart and taken through one of the entrances into the stadium. He knew that it was now or never. Whatever the risk to himself, he had to act straight away. Marcus made to come with him, but Worm put out a restraining hand.

"Not your problem," he said, hoping his serious manner would get the message across, even if his words couldn't. He offered his hand to shake and Marcus clasped it firmly before embracing him. "Goodbye and good luck, my friend – and thank you."

Marcus said something too that Worm took to mean more or less the same thing. He gave the thumbs-up sign again in gratitude and Marcus responded, forcing a grin of encouragement. Worm turned and trotted away before

either of them could change their mind or his own courage failed him.

He glanced back as he heard some commotion behind him. Marcus had upset a stall to create a diversion and then disappeared into the crowds.

"Thanks again, Marcus," Worm murmured, picking up a large jar standing against the wall. He carried it through the entrance into the amphitheatre as if helping with deliveries.

It felt like he was entering the lion's den. Worm gulped. He probably was.

8 Take a chance

In the heat, the air underneath the stadium was foul, reeking of sweat, animals and fear. There was a maze of dark passageways, lit only by small lamps, and Worm began his frantic search. Growls and snarls came from behind the first barred doors he approached and he hurried on.

Inside another of these cramped cells lay four terrified boys in soccer shorts, caught up in a nightmarish time warp beyond their understanding.

"What's going to happen to us?" whimpered Dazza, rubbing his sore arms where the chains had been. He wasn't surprised that nobody answered.

"Wonder where Worm is now?" Stopper said. "Reckon he got away?"

Jacko shrugged. "Who knows? At least if he ever manages to get back home, he'll be able to tell people how we disappeared."

"Who'd believe such a crazy story?" Ryan muttered and then gave a heavy sigh. "Guess this is it, guys. No hope of escape now."

"I wouldn't say that!"

The voice came through the narrow, barred gap near the top of the door. They recognized it instantly and jumped to their feet.

"Worm!" they chorused.

"Never thought I'd be so glad to hear you again," cried Ryan. "How did you get here?"

"No time to explain. Is it just you lot in there?"

"No, we've invited the Emperor for lunch," snorted Dazza. "Just get us out, will you!"

All the doors had their key hanging by a nail on the wall. Checking the passage was clear, Worm fitted the key in the lock and clunked it open. He was swamped by his teammates as if he'd just scored the winning goal.

"Which way do we go?" Jacko demanded.

The choice was made for them. A soldier appeared and broke into a run as he saw the slaves. He shouted a challenge and drew his sword.

"Don't reckon he's after our autographs!" yelled Stopper. "C'mon, get going. There's light up ahead somewhere."

The Rangers fled, brushing an animal-keeper out of their way. Reaching a corner, they turned towards the light.

"Oh hell!" cursed Ryan. "It's the arena. We're trapped!"

"It's our only chance," shouted Worm. "Run like mad straight across. Maybe we can get out the other side before anybody catches us."

"Or any*thing*!" added Dazza, his face deathly white.

They charged out into the harsh sunlight and the crowd roared at the apparent start of the entertainment. A large net was suddenly cast over the slaves from above and they stumbled and fell on top of one another, becoming more and more entangled.

They rolled over and over ... blue sky ... brown sand ... over and over ... blue ... brown ... blue ... green...

Hoots of laughter gradually reached their ears.

"Get a load of Worm! He's wearing a dress!"

"Where did you get that filthy old thing?"

The five boys sat up and stared around in a daze, trying to reorientate themselves. The plastered walls of the arena and the tiered seating had vanished beneath grassy mounds. And the mocking taunts came from a group of sunbathing footballers.

Gingerly, the travellers rose shakily to their feet and staggered forwards on jelly legs. Worm tore off his brown tunic and stuffed it under his arm as the Rangers' managers strode across the arena.

"What on earth...?" began Mr Thomas, seeing all the cuts, grazes and bruises on their bodies. "I don't believe it!"

"We told you not to let that fighting get out of hand," said Mr Stoppard in astonishment. "What a state you're in! You look half dead."

"Feels a bit closer than that, Dad," Stopper confessed. "We went further than intended."

"I don't know. We close our eyes for five minutes and this is what happens. What about our match tomorrow?"

Ryan had managed to recover his sense of humour. "Might have to make it seven-a-side."

The time-travellers used the leisure centre's facilities to clean themselves up and also received some first aid for their various wounds. A hot shower had never felt so good. They were in no fit condition, however, to join in the swimming.

"Is it too much to ask where our ball is?" Mr Thomas said sarcastically when they reappeared at the poolside.

"It got left at the villa," Ryan said without thinking.

"No, it didn't. We had it with us at the amphitheatre."

"Ah, right. Er ... soz, perhaps it's still there, then."

His dad sighed wearily. "No use going

back for it now. We'll never see that one again."

By the time the Rangers returned to the campsite, it was early evening and Worm rushed to the dig. He was relieved to see the archaeologists were still there, trying to make the most of the limited time they had left to find evidence of Solford Villa.

"Any luck yet?" Worm called across to the pony-tailed student.

"'Fraid not. Drawn a blank again today. Just about to pack up. I'm beginning to fear we're wasting our time here."

"Maybe not elsewhere, though," Worm said with a grin. He went into the site, nonchalantly flipping a coin in the air.

"What have you got there?"

"Found it not far away. Thought you might be interested."

He tossed it to the student who could

scarcely believe his eyes. "Amazing! This is almost as good as new."

"Is it genuine?" Worm asked innocently.

"I'd bet my degree on it. It's a silver denarius of Emperor Septimius Severus."

"When was he around?" Stopper chipped in, arriving on the scene with the other travellers to back Worm up.

"Oh, late second century, early third. Must be a freak chance that it's so well preserved."

"I'll show you where it turned up if you promise you'll have a little sample dig there tonight," Worm said cheekily. "We're leaving tomorrow."

"I'm supposed to be going out later. Got a date."

"Tell you what," laughed Ryan. "Let's toss the coin and see who wins – the villa or your girlfriend!"

Stopper picked up the idea. "Yeah, tails you keep the coin, heads we take

you to the place to find lots more of them."

"Hey! That's my coin you're gambling with," Worm protested.

"All in a good cause," said Jacko. "You want the villa saved or not?"

The archaeologist spun the coin high and they saw the head of Severus plop into view on the ground. Worm was quick to reclaim it.

"OK, c'mon, got nothing to lose, I suppose – apart from my date," the man sighed. "I'll just fetch a couple of the gang and some tools."

"Wouldn't mind if the villa did get bulldozed after what we've all been through there," muttered Dazza when he'd gone. "How will we know where to tell them to dig?"

"Easy!" grinned Jacko. "If you'd trudged up from the river carrying water as many times as I have recently, you'd know too. Reckon I could do it blindfolded. I even counted how many steps it took."

Jacko retraced those steps from the River Sol, starting from a point on the bank near the outcrop of rocks. When he halted, he found himself only thirty metres short of the soccer pitch and level with their own tents.

"Er, I was just scrabbling about in the hedge this morning," Worm said lamely, "and, um, there the coin was in the soil."

The student didn't seem very convinced by the explanation. "If this is some kind of practical joke, lads..."

Despite his reservations, the archaeologists began to dig, arousing the curiosity of more of the footballers who gathered round to watch them at work. Already, quite near the surface, a spade had clunked against stone.

In the fading light, they started to delve down more carefully with trowels. A bronze ring and a few pieces of broken pottery were removed from the earth and then another Roman coin.

"I think we could well be on to something here," the student said, unable to conceal his excitement. "We'll have to go at this much more slowly in the daylight. You know, I have a feeling we might just win our battle against the road builders yet!"

"The Villa team will have to find a new home, whatever happens," Dazza murmured. "Their pitch is doomed whether the road's stopped or not."

"Hello, this is strange," exclaimed one of the diggers. "Take a look at what I've just found!"

Handling the fragile item extremely gently, she turned and showed the audience what had emerged from the depths. A narrow strip of leather.

"I don't think it's part of a shoe," she said, puzzled, and then made a joke. "Unless it's off a football boot!"

She was nearer the truth than she realized. Worm peered at some faded lettering on the ancient leather. "Looks like it says MITRE!" he gasped.

The travellers looked round at each other, open-mouthed.

"Er ... better go and tell Dad we've got our ball back," Ryan grinned.

TIME RANGERS

Join the Time Rangers on their pre-season soccer tour and see more than you bargain for...

6. A Sting in the Tale

Ryan kicked the ball out to Will on the wing, who found himself closely marked by two opponents. He needed help.

"O Jacko, Jacko! Wherefore art thou, Jacko?" Will cried out.

The captain ran up in support, but Will had somehow managed to wriggle free. He dribbled off with the ball away from the pitch, hotly pursued by one of his schoolfriends.

Rakesh rolled about in a fit of giggles. "Did you hear what Will came out with then? It was worth travelling all this way just for that."